A Royal Wedding

Julie Tang

READ ALL THE CANDY FAIRIES BOOKS!

Chocolate Dreams

Rainbow Swirl

Caramel Moon

Cool Mint

Magic Hearts

Gooey Goblins

The Sugar Ball

A Valentine's Surprise

Bubble Gum Rescue

Double Dip

Jelly Bean Jumble

The Chocolate Rose

COMING SOON:

Marshmallow Mystery

Frozen Treats

Candy Fairies

Super Special

A Royal Wedding

HELEN
PERELMAN

ILLUSTRATED BY
ERICA-JANE WATERS

ALADDIN
NEW YORK   LONDON   TORONTO   SYDNEY   NEW DELHI

This book is a work of fiction. Any references to historical events, real people,
or real places are used fictitiously. Other names, characters, places, and events
are products of the author's imagination, and any resemblance to actual events
or places or persons, living or dead, is entirely coincidental.

ALADDIN

An imprint of Simon & Schuster Children's Publishing Division

1230 Avenue of the Americas, New York, NY 10020

First Aladdin paperback edition October 2013

Text copyright © 2013 by Helen Perelman

Illustrations copyright © 2013 by Erica-Jane Waters

Also available in an Aladdin hardcover edition.

For information about special discounts for bulk purchases, please contact
Simon & Schuster Special Sales at 1-866-506-1949 or business@simonandschuster.com.

The Simon & Schuster Speakers Bureau can bring authors to your live event.
For more information or to book an event contact the Simon & Schuster
Speakers Bureau at 1-866-248-3049 or visit our website at www.simonspeakers.com.

Designed by Karina Granda

The text of this book was set in Berthold Baskerville Book.

Manufactured in the United States of America 0813 OFF

2 4 6 8 10 9 7 5 3 1

Library of Congress Control Number 2013944081

ISBN 978-1-4424- 8898-4 (pbk)

ISBN 978-1-4424-8899-1 (hc)

ISBN 978-1-4424-8900-4 (eBook)

For Samantha,
who had the sweet idea
for a royal wedding

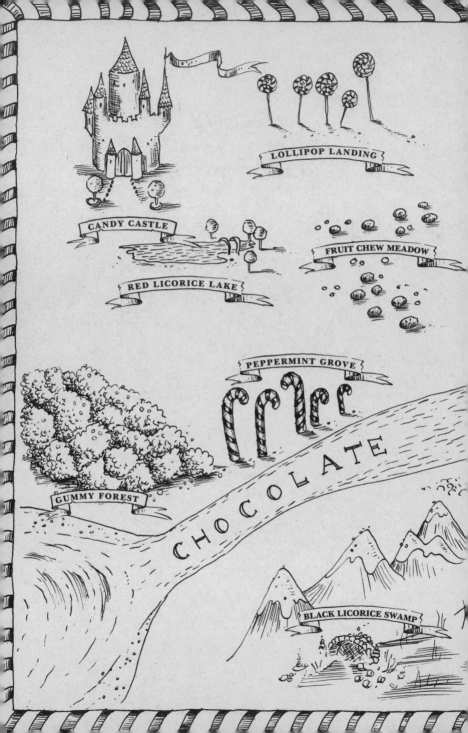

Contents

1

The Big Scoop

Melli the Caramel Fairy swooped down to the sugar sand beach at Red Licorice Lake. The sun was slightly above the top of the Frosted Mountains. She knew she was early for Sun Dip and her friends wouldn't be there for a while. Sun Dip didn't officially start until the sun started to sink behind the

Frosted Mountains. Melli fluttered her wings. She couldn't wait to share her news!

Spreading her blanket, Melli smiled to herself. She had made fresh caramel hearts for a Sun Dip snack and displayed them on a plate. Sun Dip was her favorite time of day. The colorful sunset in Sugar Valley was the perfect time to be with friends. And Melli had the best four friends in the world.

She didn't have to wait too long for her Chocolate Fairy friend Cocoa to arrive. Cocoa's golden wings were easy to spot in the late afternoon light.

"Hi, Cocoa!" Melli called.

"I thought I was going to be first today," Cocoa said. She looked at her friend. "You look like you are bursting with some sweet news."

Melli giggled. "I am!" she squealed. "The most delicious news!"

"Hold on!" Raina the Gummy Fairy cried from above. "*I* have the most scrumptious news of all!"

Dash the Mint Fairy whizzed past Raina and landed next to Melli. "Gee, everyone is extra-early today," she said. "What's the great occasion?"

"They have news to share," Cocoa said, nodding to Melli and Raina.

"Well, spill!" Dash said as she settled down on Melli's blanket. "Please don't tell me we have to wait for Berry."

Berry the Fruit Fairy was almost always late to events. Her friends knew this about her and always expected her to be the last one to arrive.

"She's probably trying on some new outfit," Dash said. Dash was more interested in sledding and speed racing than in all the fashions that Berry liked to talk about.

"Maybe," Cocoa said. She looked over at Melli. "I don't think Melli and Raina are going to be able to wait. Go ahead, Melli."

"Hey!" Raina shouted. "I have huge, huge news!"

Dash pointed her wings at Melli. "But Melli was here before you. She should share first."

Sitting up straight, Melli grinned. "Well . . . ," she said slowly. She wanted to savor the moment. "Princess Lolli wanted to work on a new caramel-apple dipping technique for the Caramel Moon Festival," she said. "And she chose me to help!" Melli's wings flapped and she lifted off the blanket. "I am going to Candy Castle in a couple of weeks so I can meet with her. Today I have been trying different kinds of caramel for the dip."

Cocoa flew over to her friend and gave her a tight squeeze. "I am so proud of you!" she said. She knew Melli loved the fall festival, which happened during the full moon in the tenth month of the year. One night of the year, the candy corn crop was picked under the full Caramel Moon and there was a big festival celebration.

"You are so lucky," Dash told her. "It's not

often that anyone gets alone time with Princess Lolli."

"I know." Melli giggled. "I can't wait."

Raina smiled. "That's great, Melli."

Dash looked down at the plate in front of Melli. "Are these fresh caramels?" she asked.

Melli laughed. Dash might be the smallest fairy, but she had the largest appetite. "Yes," she replied. "I couldn't use this batch for the dipping because the caramel was too hard, but it was perfect for shaping hearts."

"Yum!" Dash said. "I think I am going to love this special project of yours," she added.

"I will be making lots of caramel," Melli said proudly.

Raina stood up. "Now it is time for my news!" she exclaimed. "I'm sorry Berry still isn't here, but you are not going to believe this announcement."

"Announcement?" Cocoa asked. "What are you talking about?"

Raina took a deep breath. "I was at Candy Castle this morning," she said. "And I saw this!" She took out a copy of the *Daily Scoop*. "It's a special edition because this news is so delicious!"

Dash, Melli, and Cocoa crowded around the newspaper that Raina laid on the ground before them.

"Holy peppermint!" Dash cried.

"Hot chocolate!" Cocoa exclaimed.

Melli's mouth just hung open. She couldn't speak.

On the front page of the newspaper was

a large photo of Princess Lolli and Prince Scoop. The headline across the top of the paper read A ROYAL ENGAGEMENT!!

"Can you believe Princess Lolli is engaged

to be married?" Raina cooed. "Isn't that the dreamiest thing ever?"

"'The fairy princess is going to marry the fairy prince of Ice Cream Isles,'" Cocoa read aloud. "'Prince Scoop is the son of Queen Swirl and King Cone. There has not been a royal wedding in Sugar Valley since Princess Lolli's parents, Queen Sweetie and King Crunch, were married. This is going to be a supersweet celebration.'"

Berry had landed next to Raina, her large pink wings fluttering to a stop, just as Cocoa read the headline. Now her smile disappeared from her face. Cocoa turned to her. For someone who had just heard about Princess Lolli getting married, Berry didn't look as happy as she'd expected.

"Berry, did you hear Raina's news?" she asked.

Berry grimaced. "It's not Raina's news," she said. "It's Princess Lolli's news!" She turned to look at Raina. "When did you hear? The engagement was announced just today."

Raina pointed to the newspaper. "I was at Candy Castle this afternoon and I got the latest issue. Hot off the presses!"

Berry reached into her bag and pulled out her copy of the special-edition *Daily Scoop*. "I got the same news," she said. "Only, you got to tell everyone first," she added quietly.

"Raina really scooped you with the news about Scoop," Dash teased.

Everyone laughed but Berry. She didn't think that was so funny. She had wanted to

spread the news of Princess Lolli's wedding. A royal wedding was a very big occasion. Her head was spinning with fashion details and all that sugary royal glamour!

Melli wasn't as excited as her friends. "Has anyone met him?" she asked. She raised her eyebrows. She was very suspicious.

"If Princess Lolli loves him, then he has to be sure as sugar," Cocoa stated.

"The wedding will be pure sugar," Raina added. She gazed at the photo in the newspaper. "Don't they look so sweet together?"

"I've never been to a wedding," Cocoa said. She reached for one of Melli's caramel hearts.

"I hope we're invited to the wedding!" Dash blurted out.

"Of course we'll be invited," Berry said

12

with a sigh. "I think the whole kingdom will be invited. This wedding is going to be *sugartacular*!"

Raina shook her head. "Not everyone is invited to a wedding. I am sure the guest list is not as big as you think."

"Maybe they won't want young Candy Fairies there," Melli said softly. "Maybe the guests will all be royalty."

Berry stood up. "Princess Lolli wouldn't do that," she said. "She loves us!"

"When Queen Sweetie and King Crunch were married, there was a grand procession throughout Sugar Valley," Raina said. "I read all about their wedding in the Fairy Code Book. Most Candy Fairies got to see the royal couple in the parade and not at the wedding ball." She took out the book from her bag. Raina loved books and always carried the large history book. It often gave the fairies advice for their problems. "Here's a picture of their wedding," she said, pointing to one of the book's first pages.

"That was a long time ago," Cocoa said.

"Look at her dress," Berry commented. "I love the candy jewel beading, and that fabric is just delicious!"

"What will we give to the new royal couple?" Raina asked as she closed the book. "We have to give them a royally good gift even if we aren't invited to the wedding."

Cocoa jumped up. "Yes, something chocolate and gooey."

"Or rainbow and chewy," Raina said.

 14

"Sugary, for sure," Berry added. "More important, what are we going to wear? This will be the fashion event of the year!"

"*If* we are invited," Dash said, rolling her eyes.

Melli shifted her wings. "How is Princess Lolli going to have time to work on the caramel project?" She looked around at her friends. "Caramel Moon is in four months."

Cocoa put her arm around Melli. "I'll bet the wedding is after Caramel Moon," she said. "Usually weddings take a long time to plan."

"Especially a royal wedding," Berry added.

Melli wasn't so sure. As her friends continued to talk about wedding plans, she couldn't help but feel a little bitter.

2

Wedding Wishes

The next week at Sun Dip, Raina was flipping through a wedding history book, *Sweet Occasions*. All the fairy friends were at Red Licorice Lake and enjoying the purple light at the end of the day.

"There is still no news of when the wedding

will be," Cocoa said. She spread her legs out on her blanket.

"I hope the wedding is after Caramel Moon," Melli said wistfully. She drew circles in the red sugar sand with her fingers.

Cocoa leaned over Raina's shoulder. "What are you reading about?" she asked.

"There is an old Candy Fairy tradition for weddings," Raina said. "I read about it here." She held up the thick white book. "Every bride is supposed to fly down the aisle with three treats." She pointed to the book. "'Something sweet, something swirled, and something twirled.'"

"So mint!" Dash cheered.

"I wonder what Princess Lolli will do for

 17

each of those treats," Berry said. "I bet she chooses candy from Lollipop Landing or Fruit Chew Meadow."

"That's because you are a Fruit Fairy," Cocoa said. "There is plenty of fancy stuff in Chocolate Woods or Gummy Forest."

"And don't forget Peppermint Grove and Marshmallow Marsh," Dash added.

Raina agreed. "That's the fun of the tradition," she said. "Each bride can pick what is special for her and her groom."

"I did hear that Princess Sprinkle is going to be the maid of honor," Cocoa said. "I love that she chose her sister. I hope when Mocha gets married she picks me to be her maid of honor." Cocoa's older cousin lived near the Royal Palace and tended to the gardens there.

Melli started giggling. "Can you imagine Cara being my maid of honor? I can't imagine!"

"Why not?" Dash asked. "I wish I had a sister. Either a big one or a little one."

"You have us," Berry said, reaching out to squeeze Dash's hand.

Dash smiled at Berry. "I never realized how much you have to decide when planning a wedding," she said.

Berry held up her hand, touching each finger as she listed the decisions. "There's the dress, the location, the food, the cake—"

"And the ceremony," Raina interrupted. "I wonder what Princess Lolli and Prince Scoop will choose to dip at the ceremony."

"What do you mean?" Dash asked.

"During the ceremony, the bride and groom dip something into a bucket of chocolate, caramel, marshmallow . . . anything sweet," Raina explained.

"They dip the treat together and then each take a bite," Berry added. "Isn't that so sweet and romantic?" She swooned.

"Maybe they'll pick caramel," Melli said softly.

"Do you think there will be ice cream?" Dash asked. She licked her lips.

Raina giggled. "Good point," she said. "The prince of Ice Cream Isles is sure to have plenty of ice cream at his wedding."

The fairies couldn't stop talking about all

the plans and treats at a wedding. They had taken part in festivals and parties, but they'd never known anyone—especially a princess—who had gotten married. They had only read about weddings or heard other fairies telling stories.

"I wonder what the princess is thinking about now," Dash wondered. "I'll bet she's thinking of what kind of cake she'll have at the ball. She's lucky that her sister is the ruler of Cake Kingdom! Sure as sugar, that is going to be a *sugar-tacular* cake!"

Berry shook her head. "All brides are focused on their dress," she said. "It can take months to create the perfect wedding dress."

"I don't think I would care so much about the dress," Dash said thoughtfully.

"Me neither," Cocoa said. "I'll bet Princess Lolli is thinking about how dreamy her life will be with Prince Scoop and making lots of wedding wishes."

Raina closed the book and patted the silky cover. "I'm sure Princess Lolli is thinking about all the details for the ceremony," she said.

"Sure as sugar, she's not thinking about *us*!" Melli blurted out. Her face felt hot and her fists were clutched in tight balls.

Her sudden outburst caught her friends off guard. Melli was usually quiet and sweet. This was not like her at all. Cocoa spoke first.

"Did something happen, Melli?" she asked.

With everyone looking at her, Melli started to feel bad. She was happy for Princess Lolli, but she was annoyed with the timing of this royal wedding news.

"Did you get some sour news?" Dash asked, inching closer to her.

"My special meeting with Princess Lolli about my caramel apple project was canceled," Melli said softly.

"I guess she is too busy now with all the wedding planning," Cocoa offered.

"She'll reschedule," Berry said.

"Yes," Raina added, "don't worry, Melli. Princess Lolli won't forget. The caramel project sounded too delicious to forget."

Melli hung her head. "I'm not sure about that," she said. "All these big new plans . . . Everything is going to change."

There was silence. Only the faint chirping

of some caramella birds could be heard in the distance. Soon the weather would be turning colder and crops would be harvested. Autumn was always a season of change. But Princess Lolli's getting married was perhaps the biggest change that the Candy Fairies had ever known.

"Maybe things will be even sweeter around Candy Kingdom," Dash offered.

"Maybe they will get married around Caramel Moon," Cocoa said. "Melli, you love that time of year. It will be even more magical this year with a wedding."

"It was supposed to be the season for my candy project," Melli muttered.

"I think the wedding will be after Caramel Moon," Raina said. "There are too many plans to make. A royal wedding takes time to plan."

"Everyone has such sour faces!" Berry exclaimed, looking at her friends. "There's a royal wedding happening. We're supposed to be rejoicing!" She stood up. Reaching into her bag, she pulled out a notebook filled with her dress designs. "I've even been working on my dress for the wedding."

"Berry, we haven't been invited yet," Raina told her. "No invitations have been sent."

"Well, I want to be prepared, just in case," Berry said with a glimmer in her eye.

"Any excuse for a new dress," Dash said. "But I would really like to be at the Royal Palace for a piece of the wedding . . . cake!"

Dash's giggling got all the fairies laughing.

They huddled together to watch the sun glide behind the Frosted Mountains. As they sat together they each tried not to think of all the many changes coming their way.

CHAPTER 3

Swirling

Raina and Berry were tending to the lollipops of Lollipop Landing at Red Licorice Lake. About a month had passed since the news of the royal engagement. There was a shift in Candy Kingdom as everyone got ready for the upcoming royal wedding.

The two Candy Fairies were working

together on the rainbow flavors of a new crop
of swirled lollipops.

"Wasn't the engagement party invitation
the sweetest?" Berry remarked as they worked.
"What a *sugar-tastic* party that is going to be! I
knew we'd be invited!"

"We were invited to the engagement
party, *not* the wedding," Raina said. "The

engagement party is much larger than the wedding. I am pretty sure the whole kingdom was invited."

"We haven't been invited to the wedding *yet*," Berry said with a smile. "Those invitations haven't gone out." She sprinkled some fruit nectar around the stems of the lollipops. "It's impressive how quickly the wedding planning is going."

"I think Princess Lolli wants to try to get married around Caramel Moon," Raina said. "I read that in the *Daily Scoop*."

Berry flew over to another lollipop patch. "I think it's supersweet that Princess Lolli wants to be married under the big romantic caramel moon," she said.

"This is going to be hard for Melli," Raina

added. "Not to mention all the fairies trying to plan the wedding. Caramel Moon happens in about three months."

"When you are a princess, I guess plans come together fast." Berry chuckled.

"Even so," Raina said, tending to a small lollipop. "There is still not a lot of time."

Berry gently touched a light-pink lollipop. "This is like the color of the engagement invitation!" she exclaimed. "I wonder if pink is the wedding color."

"The sugar parchment was the perfect shade of pink," Raina said. "Princess Lolli has the best taste." She flew over closer to Berry. "And I loved how there was a lollipop and an ice cream cone on the top. It's so Princess Lolli and Prince Scoop!"

"As if you know him so well," Berry said, laughing.

Raina stood up and put her hand on her hip. "Well, I know he must love ice cream. He is, after all, the prince of Ice Cream Isles."

Berry laughed. "You're right," she said. She pulled some salt weeds from around a thin lollipop stick.

"Still, I am excited to go to the castle for the engagement party. I can wear my new dress!"

"I'm sure you'll look great. But I can't wait to meet Prince Scoop," Raina said.

"I know!" Berry agreed. She poured fruit nectar around the lollipops stuck in the soil. "I have only seen pictures of him. I bet he is really nice. All the newspaper articles make him seem so special."

Raina watered one of the smaller lollipops. "He must be special if Princess Lolli is going to marry him."

"Sure as sugar!" Berry agreed.

The two Candy Fairies were working busily and didn't notice that Queen Sweetie had landed nearby at Red Licorice Lake.

Berry tapped Raina's arm when she saw there were two visitors. They both watched Queen Sweetie and another fairy walk around the red sands of the lake. "Lickin' lollipops!" Berry exclaimed. "What do you think Queen Sweetie is doing here?"

Raina floated up to get a better look. "Who is with her?" she asked. "Should we go over and see?"

When the two fairies flew closer, they heard

Queen Sweetie say, "This is the location."

"I can see why Princess Lolli has been so sure about her decision," the other fairy said. "This beach does have a certain magic to it."

"Is this where Princess Lolli wants to get married?" Berry burst out. She couldn't keep her excitement in any longer.

Queen Sweetie turned and smiled at the young fairies. "My daughter is very seriously considering this location," she said. "What are your names?"

Raina hit Berry's arm. *Where are our manners?* she thought. She quickly curtsied and bowed her head. Berry followed.

"I am Raina the Gummy Fairy," Raina said.

"And I am Berry the Fruit Fairy."

"Aha! My Lolli has spoken about you. It is a

sweet pleasure to finally meet you," the queen said. "I have heard many fine stories about you and some other young Candy Fairies."

Berry's face grew warm from the praise. She turned to look at Raina, who was glowing a cherry red. *Princess Lolli has told her mother, the queen, about us!* Sweet strawberries, this was the most delicious compliment ever!

"I am Amandine," said the stylish fairy who

had arrived with the queen. "I am the royal wedding planner."

"Princess Lolli has decided to get married at Red Licorice Lake instead of at the Royal Palace," Queen Sweetie explained. "She always loved Sun Dip on the shore of Red Licorice Lake when she was a young fairy."

"Just like me!" Berry blurted out.

Raina poked Berry's arm. She was speaking to the royal queen of the kingdom! It wasn't polite to just spit out her thoughts!

Berry tried to cover for her outburst. "I mean, I think here would be a perfect place for a royal wedding," she said very politely.

Queen Sweetie nodded and sighed. "Yes, it is quite beautiful. My daughter is very sure about what she wants. And we're on a tight schedule! Lolli wants to be married under the Caramel Moon."

"Which is just three months away," Amandine stated with a worried brow.

The queen turned to Amandine. "Lolli was right. This will be a scrumptious setting for the wedding."

"We'd better get back to Lollipop Landing," Raina said, pointing over her shoulder. She was embarrassed to be listening in on the queen and Amandine's conversation.

"We're tending to the new rainbow-swirled lollipops," Berry boasted.

Raina sharply drew her breath in. Berry was often bold and never shy, but her Fruit Fairy friend seemed to keep forgetting whom she was speaking to!

The queen turned and tilted her head. She regarded the fairies for a moment. "Large rainbow-swirled lollipops?" she asked.

"They will be when we're done," Berry said, full of confidence.

Raina wanted to crawl under the licorice vine next to her.

"Amandine, please hand me the wedding binder," Queen Sweetie said.

The queen took the large purple book and leafed through its pages. Then she looked at the fairies and smiled. "Aha! I knew your names sounded especially familiar," she said. "It just so happens that is the next item on my list. I need to find a fresh crop of rainbow-swirled lollipops for Lolli's wedding bouquet. I am supposed to find Berry and Raina. What a coincidence," she added with a smile.

"Something swirled!" Berry blurted out again.

Raina glared at Berry. *Where are her manners?*

But Queen Sweetie just laughed. Raina thought it was the sweetest laugh she had ever heard. "Indeed," the queen said. "And you two fine fairies are the ones Princess Lolli said to ask to make her bouquet."

"Lolli thought the swirled lollipops could be both 'something sweet' and 'something swirled' for the ceremony," Amandine said.

"*Sweet-tacular!*" Berry said.

"It's the 'something twirled' I'm worried about," Amandine said, frowning. "So many details . . . so little time!"

Queen Sweetie smiled. "Don't worry, Amandine," she said. "Everything will get done."

Raina thought Princess Lolli was just like her mom. She curtsied. "This would be a tremendous honor, Your Majesty," she said.

"Then it is all settled," Queen Sweetie declared. "Lolli wants to carry five rainbow-sweet swirled lollipops."

"Your Majesty," Amandine said gently, "we have to return to the castle now for a meeting with Olivia."

Berry really couldn't contain her enthusiasm. "Olivia Crème de la Crème?" she asked.

"Berry!" Raina scolded.

Once again the queen showed only a smile. "Yes, Olivia Crème de la Crème is making the wedding dress. Do you know her work?"

"Of course." Berry swooned. "The most

exquisite dress designer from Meringue Island! I love her designs! She's the designer I would pick if I were a fairy princess bride."

Raina gasped. Berry really had spoken out of turn this time. Raina felt her face grow redder than a strawberry at harvesttime.

"Yes, she's a talented artist," Queen Sweetie remarked. "I must get back to Candy Castle. But I hope to see you at the engagement party in a few weeks. Thank you again, Berry and Raina, for making the bouquet."

"Thank you for the honor," Raina called out. She wasn't about to forget her manners!

As Queen Sweetie and Amandine flew away, Raina and Berry stood on the shores of Red Licorice Lake feeling a bit shocked and incredibly proud. They were going to be part of the honored tradition of 'something swirled' . . . and create the bride's bouquet!

Raina's shoulders relaxed as she watched the queen fly off toward the castle. She turned to Berry. "Can you believe Princess Lolli chose us for one of the wedding traditions?" she said to her friend.

"Those lollipops need to be wedding perfect!" Berry exclaimed.

CHAPTER

4

Dipping

The very next day a sugar fly arrived in Chocolate Woods and buzzed around the chocolate oaks. The tiny fly flew among the tall trees until she spotted Cocoa, who was spreading cocoa beans in her flower garden.

"What's the good word?" Cocoa asked as she took the note. The fly buzzed happily

 42

and sped off without waiting for a reply.

Right away Cocoa realized that the note had the Candy Castle seal on the outside of the envelope. Her heart beat faster. Yesterday she had gotten an invitation to the engagement party—all her friends had. Could this be a wedding invitation? Her wings fluttered and her hands shook as she opened the envelope.

Cocoa squealed. "Hot chocolate!" she exclaimed. The sugar fly's note sent her straight up into the sky. She was glad that no one else was around. She covered her mouth with her hand. She was surprised at her loud holler.

Cocoa wanted to share her news with Melli first. She sped off to Caramel Hills hoping to find her. If Cocoa didn't tell this news soon, she would burst!

In a flash Cocoa was at Melli's house.

"Melli!" Cocoa yelled. She was out of breath from her fast flight, but she had to get her news out. "Guess what? I am something dipped!"

Melli looked up at her friend. She wrinkled her forehead. "You got dipped? By whom?" She checked her friend from wing to toe. "Are you okay?"

Cocoa laughed and shot back into the air. She turned flips. "Yes!" she cried. "I am more than okay!" she sang out. "I am something dipped!"

"Something dipped?" Melli asked. And then, like a mint on a dark night, Melli's

face lit up. "You were asked to do 'something dipped' for the wedding ceremony?"

"Yes!" Cocoa said. "I just got a sugar fly message asking me to make the chocolate dip. Princess Lolli and Prince Scoop have decided to dip strawberries at the ceremony." She leaned in closer. "I read in the *Daily Scoop* that they like to eat chocolate strawberries together. I guess that is why they chose chocolate strawberries for the ceremony."

As Cocoa tried to catch her breath, she noticed that Melli was standing in front of a barrel of caramel. She had a basket of apples next to her, and she was carefully dipping each one. Melli's mouth was wide open. Her friend seemed to be frozen.

Suddenly Cocoa realized what Melli was

doing. She was practicing *her* dipping! Melli was working on the dipping technique she was supposed to be doing with Princess Lolli. And maybe secretly hoping "something dipped" would have been caramel apples. Cocoa's wings felt heavy as she sank down to the ground. She wished she could take back her words. She should have chosen to share her news differently. Her own dipping news had hurt Melli's feelings.

"I guess they didn't want to dip apples?" Melli whispered. "Or anything caramel."

Cocoa reached out to hug her. "I am so sorry, Melli," she said.

Melli backed away. "It's great news for you," she said, sniffling a little. "You will definitely get to go to the wedding now. Raina and Berry will be there too, because of the bouquet." She sighed. "I guess Dash and I can watch the procession with the rest of the fairies who aren't invited."

"Oh, stop!" Cocoa said. "There is still 'something twirled.'"

"Maybe," Melli said, biting her lip.

"Sure as sugar, Princess Lolli is not going to forget you!" Cocoa exclaimed.

Melli hung her head. "She already has forgotten."

Cocoa pulled Melli over to a caramel log and sat her down. "What do you mean?" she asked.

"She canceled two meetings with me," Melli said. "I understand she is busy planning a wedding in such a short amount of time. But Caramel Moon is three months away.

The time for caramel dipping is *now*."

Cocoa felt terrible. With all the swirling news of the royal wedding, Melli's favorite activity and festival was being overlooked.

The two fairies sat quietly for a long time.

"Do you think Princess Lolli will be different when she's married?" Melli finally asked. She looked down at her feet. "Maybe Candy Kingdom and the Candy Fairies won't be as important to her anymore."

"That would never happen," Cocoa said.

A cool breeze blew through the leaves of the trees above them. Cocoa didn't know what to say. Things around Candy Kingdom were going to change. She had never thought about what life would be like—for them— after the wedding.

"Maybe you should come to the castle with me," Cocoa said, trying to lighten the mood. "Maybe you will be more in the wedding spirit if you come. I need to pick up something from Tula."

Melli wasn't sure that was the answer, but she didn't want to be alone in Caramel Hills. Maybe Cocoa was right. If she went to the castle, maybe she'd get swept up in all the wedding excitement and feel a little bit better. Even if she wasn't invited. . . .

"Okay," she said. "Let's go."

Relieved, Cocoa reached out her hand to Melli. Her news was much sweeter when Melli was happier.

When they arrived at Candy Castle, there was lots of commotion in the Royal Gardens.

"Look!" Cocoa exclaimed. "There's Princess Lolli! And Tula, her special advisor, was with her."

"I haven't seen her since the engagement was announced," Melli said, flying up to get a better view.

"She looks the same," Cocoa noted.

Melli studied the princess. "I don't know," she said. "She seems different."

The two fairies flew in closer.

Princess Lolli was surrounded by a group of advisers. They all seemed to be trying to get her attention.

"Did you forget about the meeting with the Sour Orchard Fairies, Princess?" Tula asked her.

Princess Lolli nodded. "Oh, sweet sugar,"

she sighed. "I did. Tula, please send my apologies to Lemona and the others." She turned to leave.

"Wait!" another adviser called out. "What color, Princess Lolli?"

"Deep pink or light pink?" Tula asked.

"What about rainbow?" a taller adviser asked.

Cocoa and Melli watched as Princess Lolli looked at each adviser. Cocoa was sure that Princess Lolli would give a quick reply.

But she didn't.

In fact, Princess Lolli turned without answering and flew off to the castle.

"Why isn't Princess Lolli talking?" Melli asked. "I have never seen her not give her answer in a sure way."

"I don't know," Cocoa said, full of concern.

"You see. I told you!" Melli said. "Everything *is* going to be different."

Cocoa frowned. Princess Lolli had never been forgetful or not sure of herself. Cocoa had never seen her like that before.

"Princess Lolli has changed," Melli told Cocoa. "I knew this would happen. First she canceled our caramel meetings. Now she doesn't even sound like herself. And I'm sure she is going to forget all the Candy Fairies!"

Cocoa wondered what was happening. She put her arm around Melli. "Well, we'll have to wait and see," she finally said sadly.

CHAPTER

5

A Little Salt

"Berry, you are making me nervous, pacing around," Raina said. "Please sit down."

The fairies had gathered at Red Licorice Lake. They were dressed in their fancy outfits for the royal engagement party at Candy Castle.

The fairies were especially fluttery tonight.

Everyone in the kingdom was buzzing with excitement. The engagement party was going to be a magical evening!

Berry smoothed out her skirt. "I just pressed my new sugar silk dress!" she exclaimed. "I can't sit!" She spun around, allowing the deep purple folds in her dress to open and swirl around her. "I want to look positively perfect for the party."

"Everyone is going to be looking at Princess Lolli, not you," Raina muttered under her breath. She was sitting on a blanket brushing Melli's dark hair. She was going to put the Caramel Fairy's hair up in a fancy style with a new sugarcoated clip.

Cocoa shot Melli and Dash a look. What had just happened between Raina and Berry?

Ever since they had arrived, the two friends had been snipping at each other. Cocoa wasn't sure what had happened, but they were definitely *not* getting along. Maybe something sour was going on with the lollipop bouquet they were making.

"How are the lollipops coming along?" Dash boldly asked Berry.

Cocoa's eyes widened. Leave it to Dash to speak exactly what was on her mind!

"Fine," Berry snapped.

"Okay," Raina replied.

There was a heavy silence in the air. Dash, Melli, and Cocoa all stared at one another, not sure what to say. Berry and Raina had worked on many candy projects together and never argued.

"What is going on with you two?" Dash bravely said. "You have been barking at each other, and things don't feel right between you." She eyed her friends carefully.

"What do you mean?" Berry burst out.

Raina didn't say a word and concentrated on Melli's braid.

"Everything is fine," Berry said. "The bouquet will be sweet as sugar when the wedding comes."

"We hope," Raina added.

Her comment made Berry start to boil. "The stems will be thicker!" she shouted.

"If the rainbow color stays," Raina said through gritted teeth.

Oh, sour sticks, thought Cocoa. *This is worse than I thought.*

Melli quickly changed the subject. She didn't like it when her friends fought. "Do you think we'll get to meet Prince Scoop?"

"Oh, I hope we get to talk to him!" Cocoa exclaimed. "I've been reading all the articles about him, and he sounds delish."

"That is a quote from the *Daily Scoop*," Dash said, giggling. "There was an article about Prince Scoop being 'delish.' There will be so many fairies there. I wonder if we'll get near the royal couple."

"I'll bet Princess Lolli will be pretty busy with all those royal fairies from Ice Cream Isles," Melli muttered.

"Did you read that article about Queen Swirl?" Berry perked up. "She sounds like a double dose of fancy."

"That doesn't sound like Princess Lolli," Dash said, wrinkling her nose.

Raina stood up and admired Melli's hair. "All done," she said.

"Melli, you look delish!" Cocoa said.

"I wouldn't mind things just being the same," Melli said. She peered into the mirror that Raina handed to her. "I wish we were going to the castle to visit with Princess Lolli. We might never get to do that again."

Raina touched Melli's shoulder gently. "Some things will change," she said. "But some things won't. The way Princess Lolli feels about us will never change."

"You don't know that for sure," Melli mumbled.

"I think you'll feel better once you see her

and talk to her," Cocoa told her friend.

Melli thought about the last time she'd seen Princess Lolli. The princess hadn't been herself. The conversation she and Cocoa had overheard was circling in her head.

"She was acting very strange the last time we saw her," Melli said. "She's already forgetful, and she's not even married yet."

"Even a princess can get overwhelmed planning a wedding," Raina told her.

Melli rubbed her forehead. "What will happen once she has all those new responsibilities as a wife? She is going to forget all about us, I know it."

"You know no such thing," Raina snapped. "Melli, you have to stop talking like that."

Dash sat down in front of Raina for her

turn for a fancy hairstyle. "She's probably under a lot of pressure. I heard that Prince Scoop's parents are very proper and want the wedding a certain way."

"Oh, who wouldn't want a proper fairy princess wedding at a palace?" Berry said wistfully. She leaned back on a thick licorice stem with a dreamy look in her eyes.

"Berry," Dash said, rolling her eyes.

Raina brushed Dash's blond hair. "Even though things will be different once Princess Lolli gets married, they can still be super-sweet," she said.

"We can't just always stay the same," Cocoa added.

"Why not?" Melli said. "Everything was perfect. We all lived happily here in Sugar Valley."

"And we still will," Raina said. She put the brush down and started to braid Dash's long hair.

"If things always stayed the same, life around here would be pretty tasteless," Dash added.

"I guess," Melli said softly.

Berry stood up straight. "Well, tonight will be elegant," she said. "I am sure Princess Sprinkle will bring lots of cakes and special treats."

"We'd better hope Mogu doesn't show up," Cocoa said. A thick silence fell over the fairies. The thought of the salty troll Mogu barging in on the engagement party was so sour no one could speak.

"Oh, he wouldn't dare come," Dash said. Then she thought for another moment. "I guess he could . . . ," she said quickly.

"We'll have to be on the lookout," Raina said.

Berry put her hands on her hips. "I'll bet that old troll is licking his lips over all the sweets in the kingdom."

"Which is why we should be more careful about the lollipops," Raina said, glaring at Berry.

"Do we have to talk about this again?" Berry said. "The lollipops are fine."

"Should we talk about your dress instead?" Raina spat.

Cocoa looked over at Melli and Dash. The lollipops might have been fine, but somehow making the swirled candy had caused them to argue.

Dash picked up the mirror to admire her

hair. "Thanks, Raina," she said quickly. "You know we really do have to fly."

"Yes," Cocoa said, jumping up from the blanket. "We'd better get going."

"And can we try not to fight in front of Princess Lolli?" Dash asked. She looked right at Raina and Berry. Neither fairy replied.

Cocoa hoped the fighting would not make the evening salty. No one wanted that! She was anxious to see Princess Lolli. She hoped the fairy princess was feeling more herself and ready for the upcoming wedding.

CHAPTER

6

Royal Gumdrops

Holy peppermint sticks!" Dash exclaimed as she walked into the grand ballroom at Candy Castle. "That is some royal engagement party."

There were hundreds of tiny mint candies strung across the ballroom. The white mints made the whole room glow.

"Look at those centerpieces!" Berry cried. "Have you ever seen anything so deliciously beautiful?"

Each table was covered in a sparkly white meringue material with an extra-large ice cream cone filled with bunches of lollipops in different shapes and sizes. They were the perfect centerpieces for the bride and groom.

The fairies stood together at the front of the room.

Melli's eyes were wide as she looked around at all the fairies. "And the Sugar Pops are playing too!" She pointed to the far end of the garden.

The musical brothers, Char, Carob, and Chip were entertaining the fairies and singing. Melli loved their music and started to tap her foot.

"We should have known they'd be here," Berry said. "If I were a fairy princess getting married, I would have them here."

"But you are not getting married," Raina said. "And you are not a fairy princess."

Melli, Dash, and Cocoa all gasped. They couldn't believe Raina and Berry had brought their fight with them to the party.

"Would you two please stop?" Cocoa asked. She looked from Berry to Raina. "This is not like you two to be saying bitter things to each other. How can you be arguing on a night like this?"

A Cake Fairy flew over to them with a tray

of mini cakes. "Would you care for a tasty sweet treat?"

The Cake Fairy didn't realize that she was interrupting anything sour. There was a silence until Dash reached over and took a couple of the treats.

"Thank you," Dash said. "Did you make these? They look very good."

The Cake Fairy fluttered her wings. "I didn't make these," she said. "But I did make the chocolate cakes on that table." She pointed to a table filled with large round chocolate cakes decorated with lollipops and ice cream cones.

"*Choc-o-rific!*" Cocoa exclaimed. "I guess the theme of this party is lollipops and ice cream cones."

"I am glad you noticed," a voice said behind them.

"Prince Scoop!" the Cake Fairy said. She bowed her head and curtsied to the prince. At the same time, her tray of mini cakes teetered and toppled to the ground. "Oh, cake crumbles," she muttered. "I am so sorry."

"Not to worry," the prince said with a wide grin. He bent down and picked up the fallen cakes. "There is way too much food here, anyway."

Melli watched as the royal prince helped the Cake Fairy clean up the mess. He was both charming and sweet.

"Isn't he just dreamy?" Cocoa whispered to Melli.

Melli watched how calm the prince was as he helped the Cake Fairy clean up. He didn't make her feel bad about the spill and seemed to cheer her up. "He is not like I had imagined," Melli said.

"Really?" Cocoa asked. "I think he is just as all the articles described him. I think he is the perfect match for Princess Lolli."

Melli shrugged. In her mind, this prince was someone who was taking Princess Lolli away from her. He was also the reason that Melli was not working with Princess Lolli on dipping caramel apples. As she thought about all that, Melli started to feel a lump grow in her stomach.

Suddenly Melli felt a tug at her elbow.

"Melli," Cocoa whispered. "Say hello."

Melli didn't realize that the prince was standing right in front of her. Her friends had introduced themselves already, and everyone was waiting for her to speak.

"Hello," Melli managed to say in a low voice. She bowed her head and curtsied.

"You must be the Caramel Fairy that Lolli was talking about," Prince Scoop said.

Melli's eyes widened. Princess Lolli and Prince Scoop had been talking about her? She could hardly breathe.

"Yes," he said, looking at her. "You are the one who was going to try the caramel apple dips, right?"

Cocoa nudged Melli. "Tell him," she urged her.

Melli nodded. "Yes," she said.

Prince Scoop slapped his hand to his knee. "I knew it!" he said. "You know, I am a huge fan of caramel sauce. I was hoping to be part of the caramel-apple dipping project." He smiled at her. "If you wouldn't mind."

"Oh, she wouldn't mind!" Cocoa cried out.

"I was telling Lolli how on Ice Cream Isles, we use caramel sauce differently," Prince Scoop said. "She was curious if the technique would work with candy." He winked. "I told her that anything with caramel can't be bad. It would be perfect for the Caramel Moon Festival, don't you think?"

The fairies giggled, and Melli couldn't even manage a response. Her heart was beating so fast. She just eagerly nodded.

"But will there even be a Caramel Moon Festival this year?" Melli asked meekly.

Prince Scoop wrinkled his brow and looked at Melli thoughtfully. "What makes you think that?" he asked.

"Scoop!" Princess Lolli called. She rushed over to the group of fairies. "I see you've met my fabulous five Candy Fairies," she said.

The friends all beamed with pride.

"You look scrumptious," Berry told Princess Lolli. She hoped she wasn't gawking too much at the princess's gorgeous chiffon dress. The

details of the sugarcoated jewels on the dress were *sugar-tacular*! "This is the best party ever," Berry added. "We are so happy to celebrate with you."

Princess Lolli smiled. "Thank you," she said. "I am so glad you could be here today." She smiled at the fairies. "But just wait for the wedding!"

"You mean we're invited?" Berry blurted out.

Raina grabbed Berry's arm. *Not another outburst!* she thought. "Berry!" She gasped.

Princess Lolli smiled warmly. "How could I get married without the five of you there?" she said. She looked at the fairies and then moved closer to Berry and Raina. "My mother said you have agreed to make my lollipop bouquet. I hope you've been having fun."

Cocoa, Melli, and Dash shared a worried look. They hoped Berry and Raina would keep their bitterness to themselves tonight.

At that moment Dash spotted Mogu! He was lurking outside the ballroom by the window. The troll was definitely out of place. Dash's wings started to flutter. Her heart raced. She had to act fast!

Dash grabbed Cocoa's hand. "Excuse us," she said to the princess and prince. "We have to fly." Dash motioned for her friends to follow her.

"She must see some cake she has to try," Cocoa said, trying to cover for her friend. She was embarrassed by Dash's quick exit.

Princess Lolli and Prince Scoop laughed. "Oh, enjoy!" Princess Lolli called after them. "We'll talk to you later."

"What are you doing?" Berry spat at Dash when they were across the room. "That was rude to run off like that."

Dash pointed to the window that faced the Royal Gardens. The fairies all gasped.

"Sweet strawberries," Berry whispered. "Mogu!"

Seeing the salty troll standing outside the castle window made the five fairies shudder.

"We've got to do something quickly," Cocoa said.

"Like what?" Melli asked, biting her nails. She watched as the troll paced back and forth near the window. He was dodging behind the bushes.

"He just couldn't stay away," Raina said.

"We need to keep him away from this ball-room," Cocoa told her friends. "Come on, let's create a distraction fit for a greedy troll!"

The five friends headed out to the Royal Gardens. In a flash they had created a sweet feast for the troll.

"Well, this should keep him busy for a little while," Dash said, grinning. "After all these chocolates and sweets, Mogu is bound to fall asleep!"

Berry looked around at the candy they had made. "Let's hope this works," she said. "I want to head back to the party."

"Me too," Dash said. "I haven't gotten to eat any cake yet!"

The fairies flew back inside. They felt good about keeping Mogu busy in the garden, but they kept their eyes open. They didn't want Mogu spoiling the party.

The Sugar Pops sang, and everyone danced. The five friends kept checking out the garden. They were pleased when they saw Mogu fast asleep in a jelly bean bush with chocolate all over his face.

"Our plan worked," Cocoa said. "Sweet sugars, that was close!"

Raina looked over at Queen Swirl and King Cone. The royal couple were sitting at a nearby table. "Could you imagine Prince Scoop's parents' reaction to a troll coming to this party?" she said. "I'm so glad we saved Princess Lolli from that embarrassing moment!"

The friends sat down at a table

and took a break from dancing. They were enjoying a fancy fruit nectar when Princess Lolli and Prince Scoop came over.

"Are you all having a good time?" Princess Lolli asked.

"Yes!" the fairies all said at the same time.

Princess Lolli laughed. "We are so glad," she said, beaming. "Prince Scoop and I would like to ask you something." She pulled out a chair and sat down at the table. Prince Scoop stood behind her with his hand on her shoulder. "We would like to ask you five to be our gumdrops at the wedding."

"Us?!" Melli and Raina squealed at the same time.

"You mean you want us to fly down the aisle?" Cocoa asked.

"Dropping gumdrops?" Dash added.

"In fancy dresses?" Berry cried.

"Olivia Crème de la Crème is making the wedding party dresses," Princess Lolli said, winking at Berry. Princess Lolli took Prince Scoop's hand. "We'd love for the five of you to lead the procession down the aisle. Will you do it?"

"Sure as sugar!" the five friends answered together.

"Delicious," Prince Scoop said, grinning at them. "This is going to be a supersweet event."

As the royal couple flew off to greet other guests, the five friends stood in shock. They were going to be the royal gumdrops!

7

Sweet Stitches

The next morning Raina arrived at Lollipop Landing to check on the swirled lollipop crop. She spotted Berry talking to Fruli, another Fruit Fairy.

"Can you believe we're going to wear original Olivia Crème de la Crème dresses?" Berry gushed.

Raina rolled her eyes. Berry was already blabbing to everyone about being a gumdrop. It was an honor to be proud of—not brag about. Raina flew closer.

"Hi, Raina! What sweet news I hear," Fruli called.

Raina wished she could say that she was happy, but fighting with Berry was weighing her down. Fruli was fluttering her wings and smiling. Seeing the Fruit Fairy so happy made Raina feel even worse. She knew that this was such a joyous time in the kingdom and that she should feel honored and happy. But when she saw Berry lifting up the tent covering the lollipop crop, she wanted to explode.

"Berry!" Raina cried. "We talked about this. We were going to let the tent stay another

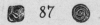

week. If we take the covering off too early, we risk damaging the sticks. The weather has been too cold for the lollipops to keep their color. It says all that in the Fairy Code Book."

Fruli stepped back. "I am going to let you two work this out," she said quickly. "I have some errands to run for Princess Lolli." She blew a kiss and shot off toward the castle. "Good luck!" she called over her shoulder.

Berry stood with her hands on her hips. "Did you have to say that in front of Fruli?" she said, glaring. "And who knows who else is around listening? I don't want Princess Lolli to hear that we've been arguing."

"Well, we wouldn't be arguing if you just listened to me," Raina snapped.

"You know as well as I do that the Fairy

Code Book is a guide," Berry told her. "Some-times crops are different."

"I know it's hard to be patient," Raina said. "But to get the right color swirl, you have to wait for the perfect time for the crop to be in the sun. It does say that in the book."

"I have made rainbow-swirl pops before," Berry said. She turned on her heel and flew off.

"We've made them together," Raina quietly added. Her wings drooped down low to the ground. She looked around. Berry was right about one thing: They had to be careful about their bickering. The last thing Raina wanted was for Princess Lolli to hear that the two of them were not getting along. Raina vowed that next time she saw Berry, she would try harder.

Later that day at Sweet Stitches, the five friends waited for their Olivia Crème de la Crème gumdrop dress fittings. Butterscotch, one of the royal unicorns, had taken the fairies over to the designer's dress shop on Meringue Island. The shop had a lavish waiting room with large couches made of the softest, silkiest fabrics.

"Feel this couch," Berry said. She pet the soft cushion. "If this is the fabric she uses for furniture, imagine what our dresses will be like!" She popped off the couch and walked around the room, gazing at the photos of different brides on the wall.

"Butterscotch was *so mint*!" Dash exclaimed. She had loved the speed and strength of the royal unicorn. The usually long trip from

the mainland to Meringue Island had taken no time at all on Butterscotch's back. She sat down on a puffy white chair. "That was the fastest ride ever. Butterscotch is even faster than Carobee," she said. Carobee was a dragon that lived in the caves of Sugar Cove. He was a good friend to the five Candy Fairies.

"I think Butterscotch might be the fastest of the royal herd," Berry agreed.

Melli and Cocoa were huddled over a fashion book with Raina on a couch across the room.

"Hot caramel!" Melli said. She pointed to a dress in the book. "Look at all the details on that dress. Those are the smallest candy crystals I have ever seen. How did she sew those on?"

"Olivia Crème de la Crème is known for her delicate candy work," Raina said. "She is very talented."

Cocoa leaned back on the cushion. "I wonder what our dresses will look like," she said. "I hope mine is as rich as a chocolate soufflé!"

"I've always wanted to wear an Olivia Crème de la Crème dress!" Berry swooned. "Do you think we'll meet her? Do you think she is here?"

"Of course she's here," Cocoa said. "This is

Princess Lolli's wedding! She is going to make sure all the dresses are perfect."

"Lickin' lollipops," Berry said. She flopped down on the couch. She stared at the closed door to the design studio. "Oh, I can't wait!"

Raina looked up from the fashion book. "Again, no patience," she mumbled.

Cocoa and Melli looked from Raina to Berry.

"What is that supposed to mean?" Berry asked. "I have lots of patience!"

"Not lately," Raina replied.

Dash sprang up. "What is it with you two?" she asked. "We're tired of hearing you snap at each other."

Melli wrapped her fingers around a strand of hair. "What is going on?"

Blowing her long bangs off her forehead, Raina sighed. She was trying not to be angry, but Berry was making her mad! "Berry is being a know-it-all," she said.

"Me?" Berry cried. "You are the one being bossy and quoting the Fairy Code Book!"

"She always quotes the Fairy Code Book," Dash said innocently.

"I know!" Berry shouted. "And it is getting annoying. The rainbow-swirled lollipops are going to be beautiful," she said to Raina. "With or without your help."

"You are supposed to be working together," Melli said softly. "The lollipops are 'something sweet' and 'something swirled.'"

"You used to love working together," Cocoa said.

"Not so much anymore," Berry mumbled.

Cocoa looked to the door. "You'd better pull yourselves together," she warned. "Don't forget where we are." She gave her friends each a stern look.

"And why we're here," Dash added.

"Raina, you don't know everything!" Berry shouted.

"I do know something about rainbow swirling!" Raina yelled.

At that moment the door to the dressing room opened. Princess Lolli walked into the waiting room with her sister, Princess Sprinkle!

The Candy Fairies were speechless.

"I thought you two would enjoy making the lollipop bouquet," Princess Lolli said. Her voice was dripping with disappointment. "But it seems to have caused you some trouble."

Raina and Berry hung their heads.

"Maybe I should . . ." Princess Lolli stopped when she saw Berry stepping forward.

"Please, Princess Lolli," Berry said. "We can make the sweetest bouquet. I know we can. We've been arguing, but we'll stop. Making your bouquet is too important."

"I'm sorry," Raina added. She looked at Berry.

"Me too," Berry said.

"Sometimes weddings make people act nutty," Princess Lolli told them. "I understand the pressure." She sighed. "Especially since we only have a couple of months before the wedding. But you should not be fighting." She smiled over her shoulder at her sister. "Ask Princess Sprinkle. We just had an argument this morning."

"But we're over it now," Princess Sprinkle said with a grin. "We had a misunderstanding. Clearing up a little misunderstanding is important before things get really messy."

"Fighting and being mad is very bitter," Princess Lolli said. "And can ruin events."

 97

A fairy with a measuring tape around her neck poked her head through the doorway. "Madame Crème de la Crème will see the gumdrops now."

"Go, gumdrops," Princess Lolli said with a gentle smile. She reached out for Raina's and Berry's hands. "Talk to each other."

"We will not let you down," Raina said.

"We'll make you the sweetest bouquet," Berry promised.

Cocoa looked back at her friends. She wasn't sure Berry and Raina had truly forgiven each other . . . or if a simple talk would solve their argument. Melli and Dash had the same concerned look on their faces. Cocoa had a worried feeling in her stomach as she followed the dress fairy into the dressing room.

8

Showers of Sweetness

Even though it seemed as if Princess Lolli's wedding was the only thing happening in Sugar Valley, there was still plenty of work keeping the Candy Fairies busy. It was harvest season, and many of the Candy Fairies were collecting candies and packaging sweet treats. Cocoa and Melli were together at the edge of Chocolate Woods taking a break from their harvest duties. They were sitting in a chocolate oak branch.

"How is the candy corn crop?" Cocoa asked.

Melli shrugged. "Better than I thought it would be," she said. "I was afraid the chill of the last couple of months would hurt the corn, but they are supersweet."

"You must be glad," Cocoa said. "What would Caramel Moon be without the candy corn harvest?"

Melli sighed. "Do you really think we'll have the Caramel Moon Festival?"

This year it seemed the royal wedding would overshadow the festival. Melli knew that the candy corn crops would have to be picked. She was sad that the harvest wouldn't be a big celebration.

"Prince Scoop was all for the festival," Cocoa said. "I heard him at the engagement party."

"He didn't actually *say* there would be a festival," Melli said. "I haven't heard any mention of the Caramel Moon Festival. I think everyone is too focused on the wedding." She looked up and saw two sugar flies hovering nearby. "For us?" she said to the small flies.

Two envelopes fell down, one for each of the fairies.

Cocoa gasped. "Oh, it's an invitation!" she cried. "We're to meet at Gummy Grove today at noon. That's right now!"

"Did you get it?" Dash shouted from above.

 101

She sped over to the branch Melli and Cocoa were sitting on. "There must be hundreds of sugar flies out delivering these messages. What could this be about?"

"It has to be about the wedding, right?" Cocoa said.

"I can't wait to find out," Dash said. "Let's head over now."

The three Candy Fairies flew to Gummy Grove. They found Raina already there. She was sitting on a rock, reading the Fairy Code Book.

"Raina, what do you think is going on?" Cocoa asked.

"Is there anything in the Fairy Code Book about this?" Dash asked.

"There are many stories about weddings

102

and traditions," Raina said, "but this has got me stumped."

Just then a herd of royal unicorns appeared in the sky. The royal families along with many other fairies landed in the grove.

"Whoa," Dash said.

Berry hurried over to where her friends were standing. She made her way through the crowd. "This is quite the royal gathering," she said. "There are fairies from all the kingdoms here."

"And only the ladies," Cocoa observed.

"Isn't this like a wedding shower?" Berry asked.

"But not very traditional," Raina said, inching forward. "Wait, Princess Lolli is going to speak!"

Princess Lolli stood in the center of the grove. A horn blew, and everyone was quiet as the bride-to-be addressed the crowd. "Thank you all for coming on such short notice today," she said. "I would like to thank my mother, Queen Sweetie, and my sister, Princess Sprinkle, for helping me make this event happen. I so appreciate you all being here. Especially Queen Swirl and her family from Ice Cream Isles. They have made quite a journey today."

"Queen Swirl doesn't look so happy to be here," Raina whispered to Cocoa. The queen was not used to being in the fields. She was still in her fancy clothes and looked a little out of place.

"Many of you know that Gummy Grove had a hard summer, with a draught destroying the crops," Princess Lolli went on. "Since this is such a happy time for Scoop and me, we wanted to give back to the kingdom. We thought we could all work together this afternoon to clear the grove and ready the ground for gummy tulip bulbs."

The fairies cheered.

"This should be a new wedding tradition," Lemona, a Sour Orchard Fairy called out. "It's a wedding shower party that will really cause something to grow!"

"I am definitely writing this up for the Fairy Code Book," Raina boasted.

"This grove will bloom with gummy flowers

in the spring," Princess Lolli told the crowd. "And all of you will be a part of that gift to the kingdom."

The castle guards lined up to hand out hoes and shovels to all the fairies.

The soil was full of hard sugar lumps. Many old vines were tangled, making the cleanup difficult. The fairies all worked hard. They wanted to make the grove bloom again for the princess and prince.

"This will be beautiful in the spring," Raina commented.

"If we can get all this out of here," Dash said, pulling on an old root stuck in the ground.

As the fairies worked, Melli saw something across Gummy Lake. She drew her breath in sharply and grabbed Cocoa's hand. She

couldn't even speak. She just pointed.

"Oh no," Cocoa said.

Dash, Berry, and Raina all looked up. They saw what had caught their friends' attention.

"Mogu!" Dash exclaimed. "Not again!"

"He just can't stay away," Berry sighed.

"Looks like we need to create another distraction for that troll," Melli said. She looked around. "I hope no one else saw him lurking by the lake."

"Let's go quickly," Raina told her friends. "Follow me. We'll go a secret way through the forest."

The friends followed Raina and arrived at the lake. Once again they served up a candy feast for the greedy troll. They carefully placed the candy in a trail that led behind three large gummy oaks.

"For sure he won't move past this," Dash said, eyeing all the candy. "And he should have a good slumber after finishing this off."

"And it will keep him out of sight from all the other fairies," Melli said.

They hid behind a gummy tree while Mogu lumbered over to the trail of candy.

"Whew," Melli said as Mogu trotted along their trail. "I don't think we'll be seeing him for a couple of hours."

"Good work," Cocoa said. "Now let's go back to the grove. We have to finish our area."

As they flew back to join the other fairies, Cocoa was happy that Berry and Raina were not bickering. They weren't exactly speaking to each other . . . but at least there were no bitter words.

"It was so nice of Princess Lolli to plan this," Raina said. "Instead of thinking of what the fairies will do for her, she is thinking of what to do for the kingdom."

"That is why she is the sweetest ruler," Cocoa said. "But we still need to think of a proper wedding gift for her."

"It has to be something unique," Berry said.

"She'll be getting so many things," Raina told her friends. "We'll have to be creative."

"Look at all those Cake Kingdom treats!" Dash exclaimed as they flew closer to Gummy Grove. From the air Dash had spotted an elaborate table set full of cakes. "I am heading over there!"

Dash's friends laughed as their Mint Fairy friend dove toward the food.

The other four landed in the field and continued with their clearing. Melli enjoyed the work—especially working with her friends. She hoped they'd be working together at harvesting the candy corn as well. . . . It was hard to imagine not picking the crops under the Caramel Moon.

At the sweets table Dash saw Queen Sweetie talking to a fancy fairy from Ice Cream Isles. Dash was amazed at the queen's jewels.

"Oh, there are still more things to get done before the wedding," Queen Sweetie said to her friend. "I do need to get Lolli to think about the wedding canopy."

"Oh yes," her friend said. "Especially since

the wedding is going to be outside. They will need to have some sort of covering. What happens if it rains? Or if the sun is glaring in their eyes at Sun Dip?"

"Princess Lolli has her ideas," Queen Sweetie said. She piled up her plate with cakes and returned to her seat. "But the wedding is not too far off. We have less than a month until the wedding date!"

Dash snapped her fingers. At that moment she knew exactly what she and her friends should get for the royal couple. But not before she sampled the treats from Cake Kingdom.

9

The Sweetest Secret

What is the big secret?" Raina asked Dash. She wasn't sure what had gotten into her Mint Fairy friend. "You've been saying you have the sweetest secret ever since we left Gummy Grove."

"Yes, tell us already!" Berry pleaded.

Dash stood on the shore of Red Licorice

Lake and looked at her four friends standing around her. "I couldn't tell you at the grove. There were too many fairies around," she said. "I had to wait till we got here."

"Please don't tell us that we have to wait for Sun Dip," Cocoa begged. "The suspense is eating at me!"

"Come on, Dash," Cocoa said. "Dish the news!"

"I finally have the perfect wedding gift idea for Princess Lolli and Prince Scoop," she whispered. "I had to keep the idea a secret while we were at the grove. I didn't want any other fairy to hear."

Berry stood up from her blanket. "There are no other fairies around here, so tell us!"

Dash smiled. "I heard Queen Sweetie say

the royal couple needs a wedding canopy for the ceremony," she said. "I told the queen that the gumdrops would create a *sugar-tastic* canopy."

Raina clapped her hands. *"Sweet-tacular!"* she yelled. "That is a delicious idea! We should make the canopy sugary colored and very fancy."

"Princess Lolli loves lollipops, and that is the theme of her wedding," Berry said. "We should make a lollipop canopy."

"And as the lollipop expert, you can tell us all how to do that?" Raina said, rolling her eyes.

"I am a lollipop expert," Berry boasted.

Cocoa, Melli, and Dash all looked at one another.

Melli bit her lip. How was this gift going to get made with her friends fighting?

Dash flew over and stood between Berry and Raina. "This is supposed to be fun," she said. "I thought you two vowed to get along."

Berry and Raina glared at each other. "It's not me," they both said at the same time.

Cocoa started to giggle. Berry and Raina each seemed so sure that she was not the cause of the fight, but Cocoa knew that a fight between friends usually involved two fairies—not just one. "I'm sorry," she said, trying to stop laughing. "You both seem sure you are not at fault, and it strikes me as funny."

"Well, it's not funny." Berry pouted. Fighting with Raina was definitely syrup on her wings.

Cocoa's laughter was contagious, and soon all the fairies were giggling—even Berry. She couldn't resist the urge to giggle along with her friends. It had been so long since she was able to laugh.

"Can you two just make up and get this fight over with?" Cocoa asked.

"Maybe you should talk things out," Melli said. "If you hear what the other thinks, maybe you can move on."

Dash took Raina's hand and Berry's hand. She brought the hands together. "Please try," she said.

Raina and Berry looked down at their clasped hands. At the same time they both smiled. "I'm sorry," they said together.

"Choc-o-rific!" Cocoa shouted.

"Princess Lolli picked you two to create her bouquet for a reason," Dash told them. "Using both of your talents is a brilliant idea."

"I think we forgot that," Raina admitted. "Berry, I just got mad when you started taking off the field tent without me. I do know about rainbow swirling."

"I know," Berry said. "I am sorry. It's just that these lollipops need to be double special.

And your quoting the Fairy Code Book was making me mad." She smiled at Raina. "I wouldn't want to work with anyone else on this bouquet. If we work together, this bouquet will be the most beautiful anyone has ever seen!"

Dash cheered and flew up in the air for a quick somersault. "Now let's get to work on a wedding present!"

"I have an idea," Melli said. "We can wrap licorice around four lollipop sticks to hold up the canopy. It can be 'something twirled'!"

Dash leaped up. "I love that idea!" she exclaimed. "We'll send a sugar fly message to the queen. She'll be so happy!"

Berry and Raina flew to Lollipop Landing to get lollipops for the canopy. Dash, Melli, and Cocoa gathered long pieces of licorice and straightened them out to wrap around the lollipop sticks.

"Princess Lolli is going to love this," Dash said. "I can't wait to see her face!"

When Berry and Raina returned with lollipops, the fairies worked quickly to decorate the sticks.

"The poles look fantastic," Melli said, admiring their work. "But what about the canopy?"

"I wish we had time to go to Meringue Island," Berry said. "There are so many fabrics there that would be *sugar-tastic* for a wedding canopy."

"Lots of fairies just use fabric," Dash told her friends. "I'd like to do something different."

Cocoa flew closer to Dash. "Hmm. Maybe we could dip some fabric into some different-colored flavors."

"We could make a rainbow swirl," Raina offered.

"What about a painting?" Cocoa asked. "I could paint a scene in Sugar Valley."

"We can't forget Prince Scoop," Dash added. "We have to have some ice cream for him." She snapped her fingers. Once again Dash had an idea. She grinned. "I have a sweet solution to our problem," she said. "What if we each make one square of a quilt? We can create our own squares and then sew them together. It will be a Sugar Valley wedding canopy quilt."

Berry hugged Dash. "That is a brilliant idea," she said.

"We should each do one square separately and then all do one together," Dash said. "If we have six squares, we'll make a perfect rectangle canopy for the bride and groom."

"I will be happy to sew the squares together," Berry said.

"Choc-o-rific!" Cocoa exclaimed.

The fairies looked up at the darkening sky. They decided to rest as they watched the sun dip lower behind the Frosted Mountains.

Dash was proud of herself and her friends now that they had a wedding gift plan!

CHAPTER 10

Mint Jitters

As the wedding day drew closer, the fairies were all extra-busy preparing for the big event. All anyone could talk about in Candy Kingdom, Cake Kingdom, Sugar Kingdom, and Ice Cream Isles was the wedding. Before they knew it, the five royal gumdrops had received word that their wedding dresses were ready!

The five friends met at the shore of the Vanilla Sea in Gummy Forest. Butterscotch was there to greet them and to fly them to Meringue Island for their dress fittings at Sweet Stitches.

"Have you heard any more about the Caramel Moon Festival?" Cocoa asked Melli.

Melli shook her head. She sat up on the unicorn's back and made room for Cocoa. "No, and the moon will be full in two weeks. The Caramel Moon Festival will be after the wedding, but I'm afraid that no one is focusing on that."

Cocoa squeezed her hand. "We'll figure something out," she said as Butterscotch took off toward Meringue Island.

Once again the five Candy Fairies sat in the beautiful waiting room at Olivia Crème de la Crème's shop. "I wonder what color the dresses will be," Berry said. "When I asked Ms. Crème de la Crème last time, she wasn't sure."

Melli flipped through a book of dress designs. "No matter what, we are going to feel like princesses," she said.

"Princess Lolli's dress has been the topic of the *Daily Scoop* for weeks," Cocoa said. "It's a huge secret! No one knows what it will look like."

The door opened and a fairy with a measuring tape around her neck peeked into the waiting area. "Ms. Crème de la Crème is ready for the gumdrop fittings," she said. "Please follow me."

Cocoa giggled as she got up from the plush satin couch. "I don't think I'll ever get tired of being called a gumdrop," she whispered.

"A *royal* gumdrop," Dash added.

The five fairies followed in a line to a large dressing room.

"Have a seat," the fashion fairy told them. "Ms. Crème de la Crème will be in to see you all."

"Sweet strawberries!" Berry squealed. "I can't wait!"

Raina smiled at Berry. "I know," she said. "What color do you think the dresses will be? Pink? Yellow? Rainbow?"

Cocoa flopped down on the seat in the center of the room. "I don't care what color the dresses are," she sighed. "It is just so nice to be here."

Dash took a handful of mini meringue cookies from a silver tray. "I could stay here all day," she said. She leaned back on the soft pillow. "A unicorn ride to Meringue Island, delicious treats, and being treated like a

127

princess are all sweet to me."

Her friends laughed and joined Dash in a little snack. The fresh meringues melted in their mouths and made the waiting not seem so bad.

"Hello, my sweets," Olivia said, bursting into the room. "I am so sorry to have kept you waiting." The famous fairy fluttered her sparkling wings and flew to the far end of the room. She took the corner of a long white piece of fabric and lifted it up in the air. "Here are the gumdrop dresses!" she said. She pointed to five delicious cotton-candy-pink outfits hanging on a rack.

Berry's mouth hung open. "Ms. Crème de

la Crème's creations are sweet as sugar!" she exclaimed.

The fairies rushed over to the rack to examine the dresses. Each one had that fairy's special candy emblem sewn on the front. There was a chocolate chip, a mint candy, a gumdrop, a caramel, and a sugarcoated fruit slice.

The fairies slipped on their dresses and Olivia smiled.

"Sweeties," she cooed. "You look delicious! Princess Lolli is a very lucky bride to have such lovely gumdrops to attend to her." She flew over to her assistant, who was holding a large box. "Here are your baskets, " Olivia said. "You simply hold the basket in your left hand and toss the gumdrops along the sides of the aisle with your right hand."

Berry couldn't help but take a trial flutter, pretending to throw out gumdrops.

"Berry," Raina said, grinning, "you do that very well."

"I've been practicing with fruit chews at home," Berry said, blushing a bit.

Suddenly Dash's blue eyes were wide and full of panic. She sat down on the couch. "We have to fly down the aisle in front of everyone staring at us? I can't do it!" she cried.

"What are you talking about?" Melli asked. "This is a huge honor."

"Dash," Cocoa said, coming to sit next to her, "you are always in the spotlight when you race. Think of this in the same way."

Dash looked up at her friends. "I am wearing

goggles and speeding by the crowds. . . . This is so minty different!" she yelped.

Olivia's assistant came back into the room. "Excuse me, we need this room," she said. "Queen Swirl is here for her fitting. Would you please hang your dresses back on the rack?" She turned and flew quickly out of the room.

"I guess we only get to be princesses for a short time," Melli muttered.

The fairies undressed and quickly got back into their own clothes. Dash was very quiet, and her friends all shared worried glances. They had never imagined that Dash would feel so nervous about flying down the aisle.

"It's just mint jitters," Raina told her. "You'll be fine."

Dash nodded. She tried not to look at her friends.

"Butterscotch is supposed to meet us at the beach," Berry said. "I suppose we should wait for him there."

As the five gumdrops left the shop, Melli suddenly realized she had forgotten her shawl inside the waiting room. "Go ahead," she said. "I'll catch up with you."

When Melli returned to the waiting room, Queen Swirl was sitting on the couch with a dress fairy.

"Excuse me," Melli said. "I forgot my wrap."

The dress fairy smiled and handed her the shawl that was draped on the chair in the corner of the room.

"Sorry," Melli said, trying to leave quickly.

 133

But before she flew out, she heard Queen Swirl make a comment that sent shivers from the tips of her wings down to her toes.

"I just don't see how they will manage in Candy Castle," the Queen said. "I didn't think Scoop would live there. He does have several responsibilities in Ice Cream Isles."

The door closed behind Melli and she tried to catch her breath. Did the queen just say the royal couple was *not* staying in Candy Castle? Would Princess Lolli leave Candy Kingdom? Melli flew straight to the dock where her friends were waiting. Her stomach was swirling as she rushed to tell her friends what she had just overheard.

CHAPTER 11

Crumbs

"Melli! You look like you saw a goblin! What happened?" Cocoa asked.

"I just can't believe what I heard!" Melli said. Her face was flushed strawberry red. "Princess Lolli is going to leave Candy Kingdom!"

Her friends froze.

"Hot chocolate, Melli!" Cocoa finally

muttered. "Who told you that piece of news?"

Melli put her hands on her stomach. She felt a little woozy. "I told you everything was going to be sour. Everything is going to change! I knew it! You see? Everything is going to be different around Candy Kingdom."

Berry took Melli's hand and brought her to one of the rock candy benches to rest. "Melli, maybe you didn't hear correctly," she said.

"Or maybe you didn't hear the whole story," Raina added.

"Queen Swirl said that she didn't think Scoop was going to manage in Candy Castle," Melli said. Tears started gushing from her eyes. "She was saying Prince Scoop has responsibilities in Ice Cream Isles."

"Princess Lolli has lots of responsibilities here," Dash whispered.

The fairies all fell silent. None of them knew what to say. Just at that moment four Cake Kingdom unicorns flew down, pulling a cupcake-shaped carriage.

"It's Princess Sprinkle!" Berry cried.

"Hello, gumdrops," Princess Sprinkle greeted the fairies. "I guess we all had dress fittings today." She looked at the sad faces in front of her. "What happened here?" She flew over to Melli and raised her chin with her finger. "Why such long faces? Please tell me this is not about your gumdrop dresses!"

"Oh no," Melli replied, snuffling. "We love the dresses."

"You don't look like happy gumdrops,"

Princess Sprinkle noted. "What has happened to make you all so sad?"

Berry stepped forward. With every ounce of courage she had, she dared to ask the question all her friends were thinking. "Is Princess Lolli . . ." Her voice trailed off, and then she took a deep breath. She started again. "Is Princess Lolli going to leave Candy Kingdom?"

"Who told you that?" the princess asked.

The five fairies looked down at their feet.

"Princess Sprinkle," Olivia Crème de la Crème's assistant called, "Olivia is still with Queen Swirl. She will be with you shortly."

Princess Sprinkle nodded, then turned back to the Candy Fairies. She smiled. "Queen Swirl told you that?" she asked.

"Well, more like I *heard* her say *something* like that," Melli confessed.

Princess Sprinkle sat down on a nearby bench. "I see," she said. She let out a long breath. "You should know that Princess Lolli cares for all the Candy Fairies very much."

"So it's true?" Dash exploded. "She's going to leave us?"

"No," Princess Sprinkle said. She looked each fairy straight in the eye. "She doesn't want to leave you, or Candy Kingdom. My sister has been feeling pressure from both kingdoms. While both kingdoms are so happy about the marriage, Prince Scoop's parents, Queen Swirl and King Cone, had very different ideas than Queen Sweetie and King Crunch about what the wedding would be like and where the couple would live."

"I can see that," Cocoa whispered.

"I am very proud of my sister and Scoop for sticking to what they want," Princess Sprinkle went on. "Planning a royal wedding has been hard." She stopped and stood up. "Change is hard for everyone, even a fairy princess—and a queen."

"We thought Princess Lolli was so happy," Raina said.

"And all the papers said how thrilled Queen Swirl and King Cone were to have their son marry Princess Lolli," Cocoa said.

Princess Sprinkle laughed. "Everyone is happy," she told the Candy Fairies. "But everyone had their own ideas. The way Queen Swirl imagined the wedding would be was not

141

what her son and Lolli wanted. And how they are choosing to live is different from some royals." She stopped and smiled. "Change can be messy at times." She sighed. "But Lolli and Scoop are going to make it work." She looked the Candy Fairies in the eye. "I know for a fact that Lolli and Scoop have decided to stay in Candy Kingdom. Princess Lolli is very dedicated to all the Candy Fairies and to Sugar Valley. She has many responsibilities that she needs to be here to attend to daily. Scoop felt that he could govern from here. He even has plans to use some ice cream techniques with candy."

Melli hung her head. She should have known Princess Lolli would never leave them. And Prince Scoop's comments about caramel sauce made more sense to her now.

Maybe there would be the Caramel Moon Festival after all. Maybe there would be even more caramel-inspired events. "Poor Princess Lolli," Melli said. "How is she now?"

"You are sweet for asking," Princess Sprinkle said. "Lolli is actually doing very well. Often with difficult changes we can't help making crumbs." A smile spread across her face. "But crumbs are good too!"

"Sure as sugar," Dash agreed.

"I hope at the rehearsal next week you can sweeten the event with some good cheer," Princess Sprinkle said. "Knowing that her Candy Fairies are happy will ease my sister's mind."

"We'll be there one hundred and choco-late percent!" Cocoa cheered.

"Princess Lolli has always been there for

us," Raina said. "We will be there for her."

Princess Sprinkle grinned. "I knew Lolli picked five very special fairies to be her gumdrops."

Butterscotch flapped his large wings overhead. Their ride back to Sugar Valley had arrived.

"Princess Sprinkle," Olivia's assistant called, "we are ready for you."

"Perfect timing," the princess replied. "I believe our business is done here," she said to the fairies. "I will see you at the rehearsal. Make sure to bring all that sweet good cheer!"

As the five Candy Fairies climbed up onto Butterscotch's back, they were all quiet.

"Do you think Princess Lolli is okay?" Dash asked.

"She always knows the right thing to do," Raina told her friends. "It is hard to imagine her upset."

"She's under some royal pressure!" Dash exclaimed.

"I bet that she is fine," Berry said. "More than fine—she's going to have a beautiful wedding, and she's marrying dreamy Prince Scoop!"

Dash nodded, but she still wasn't too sure.

As Butterscotch took off for Gummy Forest, each of the Candy Fairies felt the weight on their wings of changes ahead.

CHAPTER

12

Finishing Touches

Raina spread the newspaper clippings from the past few months out on her desk. She was working on a royal wedding scrapbook. As she reviewed the articles, she realized that many of the details of the wedding were recorded. It seemed that everyone in

Sugar Valley was hungry for details of the wedding plans.

When Raina finished gluing the articles into her book, she realized that she had better get dressed. She didn't want to miss one minute of the rehearsal. She and her friends had worked hard on their toast. They were going to show Queen Swirl and all the other fairies how much Princess Lolli meant to them . . . and how much they loved her.

Just as she was about to leave, Berry flew into Gummy Forest.

"Hi, Raina!" Berry called. She swooped down and landed next to her friend. "Ooooh, I love your dress!"

"Thank you," Raina said. "I wasn't sure if

I should wear the blue one or this rainbow one." She spun around for Berry to get the whole look of her outfit.

"Sweet-tacular!" Berry cried. "I really like the rainbow colors."

Raina grinned. "And your dress is super-sweet," she said. She had seen the fabric that Berry had selected for her dress. Raina thought the dress had turned out even better than she had imagined. "You are so talented, Berry."

Berry blushed. "Thank you, Raina." She was so glad that there was no more sour sugar surrounding her and Raina. It felt good to be back to being nice to each other and working together to make the wedding bouquet. "The lollipops are doing well," she reported. "I checked on them again this morning. We'll pick them tomorrow morning so they will be fresh for the wedding bouquet."

"Perfect," Raina agreed. "I can't wait to see Princess Lolli's face when she sees the lollipops. I think they are our finest work."

Berry reached into her shiny strawberry-shaped handbag. "I made this for you," she said. She handed a small package to Raina.

"Oh, Berry," Raina sighed. She opened the wrapping, and there was a beautiful rainbow lollipop necklace. "This is the sweetest gift." She put the dazzling necklace on. "I am going to wear it tonight!"

"I wanted to give you something," Berry said. "And to apologize to you again."

Raina laughed and took out a wrapped

package from her bag. "I have this for you," she said. "I guess we both had the same thought."

The gift was a shawl with a giant rainbow lollipop. Berry knew that Raina had spent a lot of time sewing the fabric together. "Thank you, Raina," she said. She draped the wrap around her arms.

"I think we're both ready for a royal rehearsal," Raina said. "We'd better get flying. I don't want to be late!"

The two friends headed to Red Licorice Lake, where the fairies in the wedding would be rehearsing. Cocoa, Melli, and Dash were waiting for them when they arrived.

Amandine, the wedding planner from the Royal Palace, was directing fairies. She waved the five gumdrops over to her. "Please stand here," she said. She was holding a long scroll and checking off all the fairies as she spotted them. "You will fly down the aisle, pretend to toss gumdrops, and fly up the steps to the canopy." She touched her hand to her head. "The homemade canopy that isn't ready yet," she grumbled under her breath. "But the

151

poles are set up so
you know where
to stand." Then
she stared down
at the gumdrops.
"Two of you stand
right and three stand
left down near the canopy." She gave a quick
smile and added, "Don't fly down without
a smile!" She turned and flew off to attend
to Princess Sprinkle and King Crunch and
Queen Sweetie.

Raina saw their gumdrop baskets on a
bench and handed one to each of her friends.
"Don't worry," she said. "And smile!"

"Did you catch that insult about the
canopy?" Dash growled.

"She hasn't seen it yet," Melli said, soothing Dash. "She has no idea how special the canopy is."

Amandine rang a white sugar bell. "Places, please!" she called. "I need the royal family, the ushers, and the gumdrops. Start the music!"

"She's tough," Cocoa whispered to Melli. "I hope she thinks my chocolate dip is royally rich enough. I worked really hard on getting the chocolate ready for dipping."

"I am sure it's choc-o-rific," Melli told her. She watched Amandine flutter around the wedding party. "We only get one rehearsal," she replied. She didn't take her eyes off Amandine. "Where do we stand?"

"To the left," Cocoa responded.

Amandine stood at the back of the aisle. She cued the conductor, and the music of a harp and six violins filled the air. "Come along," she said to the gumdrops as the song played. "Heads up and smiles wide!"

Berry and Raina flew down first, and Melli and Cocoa followed. Dash was the last one to fly. When she got to the end of the aisle, she stopped.

Dash wasn't sure which way to fly. Should she go right or left?

Amandine barked orders from the front aisle. "Move along," she said. "Smile and stand to the right."

Dash wasn't sure if she meant her left or Amandine's left. She looked and saw Melli and Cocoa standing to the left and Berry and

Raina standing to the right. She was stuck.

"Up you go," Amandine shouted to Dash. "We need to stay on cue."

Dash's eyes got wider, and she stood with her feet firmly on the ground.

"Go ahead," Amandine said. "You are the last gumdrop to fly."

Dash flew over and stood next to Melli and Cocoa. She barely paid attention to the rest of the rehearsal. It was only when she felt Cocoa's elbow in her side that she paid any attention.

"Look," Cocoa said. She was staring down the long aisle at Queen Swirl. "What do you think is happening?"

Dash saw Queen Swirl standing with a few fairy ladies. She didn't look happy.

 155

"I'm not sure, but I know our toast will cheer her up," Melli said brightly.

After Princess Sprinkle flew down the aisle, Amandine clapped her hands. "Perfect," she shouted. "Everyone remember your spots. And please, always keep smiling!"

"And now let's eat!" Prince Scoop exclaimed.

Everyone around Red Licorice Lake cheered. After standing and smiling for Amandine, everyone was ready for a meal. As the wedding party flew to Candy Castle, the Candy Fairies thought about their toast.

"Does everyone know her part?" Berry asked.

The fairies all nodded. Not only had they practiced, but Raina had written out their parts for them.

There was a stage in the back of the garden, and the friends flew up to the microphone. "Let's ask to go first," Raina suggested.

Dash looked around at the trays of food and sweets. "I agree," she said. "I don't think I could eat a thing until we give this toast."

Amandine appeared. "Oh good, you are here," she said. "Would you five like to go first? I know Princess Lolli would love to hear from her gumdrops."

The friends gathered around the microphone. Each one spoke her line.

"Princess Lolli," Raina began, "you and Prince Scoop make the sweetest pair." Raina raised a gummy heart.

"We wish you the sweetness of chocolate," Cocoa said, holding up a chocolate.

"With a splash of a minty good time," Dash added. She felt her face redden as she spoke in front of all those fairies!

"We will stick with you and promise to be there to help," Melli said. She lifted her jar of caramel.

Berry stepped forward with her basket of jelly beans. "We wish you both all the sweet flavors of the valley."

"Sure as sugar," the five friends said together. "We wish you every bit of sweetness for your marriage!"

Princess Lolli flew over and hugged her fairies. "That was pure sweetness," she said. "Thank you."

At the end of the night the five friends were getting ready to go home. Dash pulled them aside. "I don't want to be a gumdrop anymore," she said. "I can't fly down the aisle."

"You spoke during the toast," Berry told her. "You were great."

"I just can't do it," Dash cried out. And she took off with great speed and left her friends standing in the dark Royal Gardens . . . speechless.

13

Simply Delicious

Early the next morning four very concerned Candy Fairies in their pink gumdrop dresses stood on Dash's porch. They shared worried expressions as Melli rapped on Dash's front door.

"Where could she be?" Melli cried. She peered into Dash's front window.

"I knew we should have come last night," Cocoa said.

Raina shook her head. "Dash needed time alone," she replied. "She wouldn't have listened to us last night."

Cocoa bit her lip. "I hope you're right," she said. "But where can she be? Today is the royal wedding! Of all the days for her not to be here!"

"I'm right here, silly sugar heads!" Dash called from above. "It's the morning of the royal wedding. It is not a day to be sleeping late!"

The four friends all looked at one another with great surprise.

"You seem to have had a change of heart," Berry said.

"What do you mean?" Dash asked.

Raina flew forward. "Well, um . . . about the wedding? You know, being a gumdrop?"

Dash hurried inside her house. "Oh, I didn't change my mind about that," she said. "I'm excited *about* the wedding. I didn't say I was excited to be *in* the wedding."

"Oh, sugar sticks," Melli said, frowning. She and her friends followed Dash inside.

Dash was busy sorting her mint candies, which she had just picked from Peppermint Grove. Her pink gumdrop dress was hanging in the corner of the room. The Sweet Stitches wrapper was still covering the dress.

"Dash, we understand how you feel and that you are nervous," Raina said.

"But we don't want to be gumdrops without you," Cocoa burst out.

"Think about Princess Lolli," Berry said.

"She'd be so disappointed."

Melli pulled Dash down to sit next to her.

"I'll bet Princess Lolli has sugar flies buzzing

in her stomach about today. Imagine how she must feel!"

Dash tilted her head and looked at Melli. "I never thought of that," she said quietly.

"She needs us by her side," Raina told her.

"Come on, Dash," Berry pleaded. "Let's do this together for Princess Lolli."

Dash took a deep breath in and out. She looked at her friends dressed in their gumdrop dresses.

"A bad rehearsal usually means a perfect performance!" Melli said, trying to sway her.

"And you know to smile wide," Cocoa said.

Dash listened to her friends. She tried not to think about how nervous she was going to feel when flying down the long aisle. She tried not to think about all the fairies in all the kingdoms watching the procession. She nodded. "I'll try," she said. "With a wide smile," she added.

"Amandine will be thrilled," Cocoa said, laughing. She rushed over to hug her friend.

Dash saw the basket at Berry's feet. "Is that the lollipop bouquet?" she asked.

Berry held up the basket. "Five rainbow-swirled lollipops," she cried.

"*So mint!*" Dash exclaimed. "Those look royally amazing!"

Raina smiled. "They came out perfect," she said, giving Berry's hand a squeeze.

"Wedding perfect," Berry added.

"We have the bouquet, the canopy, and the twirled poles," Raina said. "I think we're ready."

"The chocolate dip is done too," Cocoa added.

A sugar fly flew in through Dash's window and dropped a message in Dash's hand.

"It's time!" Cocoa exclaimed, peering over Dash's shoulder at the note. "We're being called to the castle."

"I can't wait to see Princess Lolli's face when she sees the canopy we made!" Raina exclaimed.

"I have the gift right here," Dash said. She held on to a beautifully wrapped silver sugar box.

At Candy Castle there were many fairies getting ready for the grand wedding procession and making sure that every piece of candy in the kingdom was in the right spot.

The five gumdrops were escorted up to the bridal room on the top floor of the castle. The five friends were bursting with excitement and pride. Princess Lolli had her back to the door when the fairies flew in. When she turned to greet the gumdrops, they gasped loudly.

"The dress is magnificent!" Berry exclaimed.

"The dress is so you!" Cocoa squealed. She loved how there were embroidered rainbow-swirl lollipops around the base of the full white meringue bottom.

"You look simply delicious," Melli sighed.

"Thank you," Princess Lolli said. "I wanted a chance to speak to you before the ceremony." She motioned for the group to come closer. "I was so proud of you last night. You spoke so beautifully and from the heart. Scoop and I

 167

appreciated what you said, and we're thrilled that you are going to be our gumdrops."

Melli glanced over at Dash and then squeezed her hand.

Berry and Raina stepped forward. They handed the bride her bouquet.

"Oh," Princess Lolli sighed, "these are gorgeous!" She took the bouquet of swirled lollipops out of the basket and held them up. "Thank you," she said. "And I am so happy to see that you were able to work things out between you."

The two fairies beamed.

"There will be many fairies watching today," Princess Lolli went on. "I want you all to have a good time. Do you all know where you need to stand?"

"One hundred chocolate percent!" Cocoa cried.

Princess Lolli laughed. "Well, that might be more than I can say."

Dash stepped forward and presented their wedding gift to the princess. When the bride opened the box, the five friends helped her unfold the quilt.

"This is . . ." Princess Lolli couldn't finish her sentence.

Dash glanced at her friends. Did Princess Lolli not like the gift? Was she not sure how to tell them?

"Princess Lolli?" Dash asked. "Are you all right?"

Princess Lolli nodded. "This is the most thoughtful gift," she said, wiping her eyes. "I am so touched. You worked very hard on this."

"We spoke to your mother, and she said that you could use a canopy for the ceremony," Raina said.

"And the poles are 'something twirled,'" Melli told her proudly.

Princess Lolli laughed. "That is why my mother kept telling me not to worry about the wedding canopy and 'something twirled,'" she said. "She knew I was going to have the most delicious ceremony." She reached out to hug the fairies.

"Princess Lolli," Dash said, "are you nervous?"

Raina squeezed Dash's hand. She didn't want to upset Princess Lolli or make her more nervous than she already was for her big day!

The beautiful bride smiled down at Dash.

"Honestly, I have never been so nervous!" she cried. "But so is Scoop! There are just so many fairies who want to wish us well . . . It is a little overwhelming. We're going to do this together." She looked at each of the fairies in front of her. "You are the sweetest gumdrops ever."

"Something sweet, something swirled, and something twirled," Raina recounted the wedding rhyme. She thought about all the things set for the wedding. The bouquet was swirled and sweet rainbow lollipops, Cocoa had handled the chocolate for the dipping, and now the licorice poles for the canopy were the twirled.

"What about something wet?" Berry asked. She moved over to the window. Her wings drooped down to the ground. It was raining!

CHAPTER

14

A Sweet Sign

S our sticks," Melli said with a gasp. She raced over to the window and peered down into the wet gardens.

Cocoa shot her a stern look. "Oh, don't worry, Princess Lolli," she said cheerfully. "I'll bet the rain will pass before Sun Dip."

Melli understood right away what Cocoa

was doing. She quickly changed her voice and put on a smile. "Yes, yes, the rain will stop," she said, grinning.

Princess Lolli leaned her head against the window. "People say it's good luck to have rain on your wedding day," she said. She turned around and looked at her gumdrops. "What do you think?"

"Sure as sugar!" Melli cried. "This is a sweet, lucky day!"

"Think how lush and shiny all the candy will be," Berry said, trying to sound positive. "Especially all the bulbs we planted in Gummy Grove."

Dash was biting her tongue. *What about all the soggy sugar patches and dripping candy?*

 174

Even though she was thinking that, she didn't dare say a sour word!

The doors burst open. "This calls for the backup plan!" Princess Sprinkle exclaimed. She flew into the room with Queen Sweetie and Amandine at her side.

"Everyone keep calm," Queen Sweetie declared. She glided right up to the bride. "Lolli, my sweet, your sister and I have already rolled out the rain plan."

Princess Lolli took her eyes off the raindrop-covered window. She looked from her mother to her sister. "What rain plan? I am supposed to get married on the shore of Red Licorice Lake . . . outside."

"As your maid of honor, I made sure we

took care of all possibilities. We had a tent ordered, just in case," Princess Sprinkle told her. She gave her sister a tight squeeze.

Raina stepped forward. "You once told me that even if something doesn't go according to your plan, it can still be perfectly sweet," she said. She remembered when her crop of gummies were rainbow swirled after a huge rainstorm. Princess Lolli had helped her to see that unplanned changes could make things even sweeter.

Princess Lolli laughed. "I did, didn't I?" she said. "That was good advice, yes?"

"Very good," Raina said, giving Princess Lolli a hug.

"Come on," Raina called to her friends. "Amandine said we have to take our places.

The carriage is here to take us down to Red Licorice Lake!"

Berry took a last glance in the long mirror. "Here we go, gumdrops," she said. "Are you all ready?"

"As ready as I'll ever be," Dash said.

Cocoa put her arm around Dash. "Just remember to smile wide," she said in Amandine's voice. "Think of what a great job you did with the toast."

The friends followed the princess out of the bridal room and down the grand staircase. Princess Lolli peered out the round window in the hallway.

"Oh, mother!" Princess Lolli gasped as she got outside. "The rain stopped!"

Queen Sweetie took her daughter's hand.

"This wedding is going to be delicious, don't you worry!" she said.

Just as they were all heading out to the carriages, Melli spotted Mogu. Once again the troll had shown up at the castle. He was lurking in the Royal Gardens. Melli noticed that his clothes were not chocolate stained as usual. He actually looked pretty clean.

"Mogu!" Cocoa said.

"He is holding a present," Dash whispered to Berry.

"I don't think I've ever seen him so neat," Melli said.

The troll waddled over to Princess Lolli. He extended a gift and bowed his head.

"You don't see that every day," Raina remarked.

"Do you think all those times we spotted him around Sugar Valley he wanted to give her a gift?" Melli asked.

Dash watched the troll. "Holy peppermint," she said. "I think he did just want to give Princess Lolli a wedding gift."

Mogu's gift was a braided red and black licorice bowl. Berry admired the troll's fine work. The five fairies moved in closer to hear the bride's response.

"Why, thank you, Mogu," Princess Lolli said sweetly. "This gift is incredibly thoughtful and kind. Scoop and I thank you for this gesture."

Mogu bowed and slowly lumbered away.

 179

"We shouldn't have thought the worst," Raina whispered to her friends. "I guess Mogu wanted to wish her well like everyone else in Sugar Valley."

Six sugarcoated carriages awaited the royal wedding party. A palace unicorn, wearing the finest sugar bridle, flew each of the carriages to the shores of Red Licorice Lake. The royal procession had begun!

"I can't believe we're doing this!" Cocoa exclaimed, staring out the window of the carriage.

"I know," Berry said. "I am trying to remember all of Amandine's instructions."

"Look at all the fairies who came out to wish the princess well," Raina said. She looked out the carriage window at the crowded streets

filled with fairies trying to get a glimpse of the royal bride.

As they pulled up to the lake, they saw the guards taking down the tents. The sky was clear, and everyone could see it was the start of a *sweet-tacular* Sun Dip.

Amandine greeted the gumdrop carriage. "Here are your baskets," she said, giving them each a shiny candy ice cream cone filled with candy. "The gumdrops were just picked this morning."

"Oh, they smell so good!" Dash said with her nose already in the basket.

"Remember, these gumdrops are for throwing, not eating," Amandine said.

Dash laughed. "Yes, I know," she said. "And we'll fly—"

"With wide grins," her friends all finished together.

"Gumdrops!" Amandine called to them. "Please take your places! The wedding ceremony is about to begin!"

15

Ever After

The music began, and the five gumdrops flew down the aisle just as they had practiced. When they arrived at their places, the aisle was lined with a rainbow of soft, bright gumdrops.

The altar was decorated with ice cream cones and colorful candies.

"Pure sugar," Berry said. "This is beautiful. I have never seen anything so romantic."

"And magical," Raina added.

Cocoa was proud that in the center of the platform was a large silver bowl of chocolate. The bowl was on a pedestal under the wedding canopy for the dipping ceremony.

The musicians changed the tune, and a dozen trumpeters with caramel horns lined the red licorice carpet.

"Here comes the bride!" Cocoa whispered to Melli.

Melli held her breath. She was so nervous!

Princess Lolli was beaming as she flew down the aisle, Queen Sweetie and King Crunch on either side of her. Prince Scoop, with Queen

Swirl and King Cone, met them at the first step of the altar.

The Royal Justice of the Palace Court stood in the center of the altar wearing a grape-colored robe with marshmallow trim. He smiled warmly at the couple.

"Aw," Dash sighed when the families met.

Prince Scoop reached for Princess Lolli's hand and guided her up the steps to the wedding canopy. They turned and waved at the crowd.

The crowd cheered.

The royal justice began the ceremony. Cocoa couldn't wait for the dipping part of the service!

Finally, the bride and groom were presented

with a silver tray. There was a giant strawberry for the dipping ceremony. Cocoa hoped their first bite would be sweet.

"Fruli had three other strawberries as backup," Berry whispered to Raina. "But this was the largest one."

"Wedding perfect," Raina said, winking. She knew Berry's Fruit Fairy friend Fruli would have made sure a special strawberry was used for the ceremony.

"With this dip, our bride and groom make a solemn pledge to each other," the royal justice said.

As the couple dipped the strawberry together, Cocoa was beaming with pride. This was the most important batch of chocolate she had ever made.

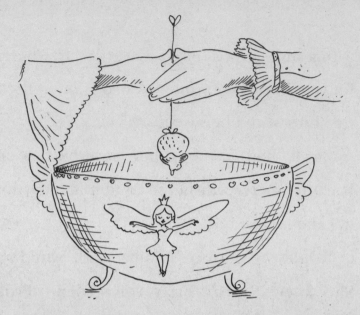

"I now pronounce you husband and wife!"
the royal justice declared.

The caramel trumpets blared once again.
Princess Lolli and Prince Scoop were married!
They flew back down the aisle together.

Berry looked up at the sky. Even though it
was almost Sun Dip and the sun was begin-
ning to set, she saw something special in the
sky. "Raina," she whispered, "look!"

"A double rainbow!" Raina said. "Sweet sugar! That is a sweet sign."

While the wedding party waited for the carriages, Raina went over to Princess Sprinkle. "How did you arrange for a double rainbow?" she asked.

"I didn't!" Princess Sprinkle said. "You see, those unplanned changes are scrumptious. The 'something sweet' can also be the throwing of rainbow sprinkles as the couple rides off to the Royal Palace for the ball. Will you and the rest of the gumdrops hand these sprinkle packets out to the guests?"

"Sure as sugar!" Berry and Raina said together.

The five gumdrops spread out and passed the packets to the fairies lining the procession path. They wanted Princess Lolli and Prince Scoop to fly away from Red Licorice Lake in a blaze of a sprinkle rainbow.

"Look how happy Princess Lolli is," Melli said. She watched the princess greet her guests.

Cocoa smiled at her friend. She was glad Melli wasn't sad anymore. Today was a day of celebration.

Prince Scoop came over to the gumdrops. "Melli," he said. "I want to make sure that we set a date so you could help me with a caramel-apple ice cream that I am working on. I want to have the project done for the Caramel Moon Festival next week."

"Hot caramel!" Melli exclaimed. "There really is going to be a festival? I would love to help out."

Prince Scoop smiled. "I knew I could count on you."

Melli smiled as Prince Scoop walked away. "I think everything is going to be supersweet in Candy Kingdom," she said.

"I think you are right," Cocoa said. "I love weddings!"

"I guess Princess Sprinkle was right," Raina told them. "Sometimes the changes that are the hardest are the sweetest in the end."

Berry pulled her friends close. "And having friends to share this with is the icing on the wedding cake!"

Princess Lolli flew over to her gumdrops and gathered them close. "Thank you for making this day extra-sweet. Cocoa, your chocolate for the ceremony was perfect.

Melli, your 'something twirled' added so much to the ceremony. Dash, your idea of the wedding canopy was so touching. And Raina and Berry, this bouquet is even grander than I had imagined." She looked down at the five lollipops. Carefully, she untied the

ribbon holding the sticks together. "I want you each to have one of these," Princess Lolli said. She gave a wedding bouquet lollipop to each gumdrop.

"Thank you," the gumdrops said at the same time. Each held her lollipop with pride.

"Something sweet, something swirled, and something twirled," Raina said.

"Sure as sugar," Berry agreed.

The royal gumdrops knew that the princess and the prince would live happily ever after.

And that was *something* to celebrate.

Candy Fairies

Chocolate Dreams

Rainbow Swirl

Caramel Moon

Cool Mint

Magic Hearts

Gooey Goblins

The Sugar Ball

A Valentine's Surprise

Bubble Gum Rescue

Double Dip

Jelly Bean Jumble

The Chocolate Rose

A Royal Wedding

Visit candyfairies.com for more delicious fun with your favorite fairies.

Play games, download activities, and so much more!